Angels Come in Strange Disguises

Mavis Thompson

Clink
Street

London | New York

Published by Clink Street Publishing 2014

Copyright © 2014

First edition.

ISBN: 978-1-909477-10-0
Ebook: 978-1-909477-11-7

Dedicated to all my lovely family and to my dear friend Helen, who has inspired me through her good humour, faith and positivity.

Where Have All the Angels Gone?

Hark the Herald Angels sing,
Welcoming the new born King
Why don't angels sing today
Appearing in their bright array?

But they do come every day
Material things just cloud our way.
They come as people, fat or tall,
Ragged, old, 'hoodies' and all!

Remember the day when tired and flat
A smiling face dispelled all that?
Perhaps another time when ill
A friend brought toddy for that chill.

These are angels, one and all,
They are permanently on call
So, if you feel alone and sad,
Just call, they'll come to make you glad.

So each day make it your goal
Be an angel to some sad soul,
In future then you'll see
Angels <u>abound,</u> in you and me!!

Angel on Board

In 1926, Eric, who was a graduate industrial chemist of Birmingham University, found himself without a job, but newly married to Kathleen. He told me of the kindness of people in those days. Life revolved around the church; it was the community, people cared for each other and Sunday was a high day, not just for everyone to 'show the flag' but also to find companionship and a meeting place. People, knowing Eric and Kathleen's plight, would leave a loaf of bread on their doorstep or a dozen eggs. They were never starving, even though there was no dole money or any other help in those days.

He was offered two jobs, one in France and the other as a lab technician in India. Kathleen resisted the idea – India was a foreign and unknown land besieged with plagues and pestilences. However, recollection of the glamorous stories his brother, who had gone there as a newly recruited army officer, had regaled him with appealed to Eric, and, having persuaded Kathleen, they duly set sail.

The journey was one of excitement and adventure for a young couple who had barely set foot out of Birmingham. As they drew nearer to their destination they became concerned. They had to journey to a place situated right in the south of India. As the ship only went to Bombay they would have to find their way south with no money in their pockets.

A kindly old gentleman whom they had befriended during the voyage heard about their plight and said, "Young man, you have been good to me and here is the money for your journey south. I would like to give it to you, but knowing your pride, I know you won't accept it, but when you can, you can pay me back. I also urge you to buy Hudson Bay shares if you are ever in the position to do so!" Eric paid him back, but was never in the financial position to take his advice about the shares, or he would have died a very wealthy man!

Eric and Kathleen lived in South India for 30 years. Eric was seconded back into the army (he was conscripted in the last year of the '14/'18 war) and was sent to Kirkee, near Poona, to use his skills as an industrial chemist in helping to make TNT, as there was a fear the Japanese would invade India. He then rejoined his company after the war. They had an exciting and full life, all their three children were born in the home, living very frugally at first until Eric was promoted to Director of the company. They lived through the transition from British rule to home rule.

They finally retired in 1960 to West Sussex. They had many enriching experiences and blessings and had a great fondness for the country in which they had served and helped. THEY NEVER FORGOT THAT PARTICULAR ANGEL WHO WAS SENT TO THEM IN THEIR HOUR OF NEED!

The Bearded Angel

Mavis was a sickly child with chronic bronchitis, suffering endless nights of coughing and inhaling Friars Balsam and being swathed in eucalyptus wraps. There were innumerable sessions of infra-red therapy taken wearing strange goggles and sitting in the weird blue light for hours. Harley Street specialists predicted that she would always be cursed with this disease. Frightening dreams ensued with noises in the ears saying, "The doctor's coming", usually caused by a clock in the room. She missed months of school and was rather pale and consequently rather a miserable child.

One day when she had been confined to bed for about three weeks with another bout of fever and coughing, her mother announced a visitor. She said he was Bishop Pakenham Walsh, who would pray with her. Mavis was slightly fearful of his visit. However, he was not the awesome figure she had envisaged, but rather like an older version of how she had imagined Jesus! He must have been in his eighties, but was well built and erect, had a white beard and piercing blue eyes and exuded gentleness and love. He sat at her bedside and said that Jesus wanted her to get better and they would pray together and he would lay his hands on her for Jesus to send his healing power. She never forgot the great feeling of peace.

When he had gone she said to her mother, "Poor man, he must have had a fever like me, his hands were burning hot." From that day to this Mavis has remained free from bronchitis!

Later she learnt from her mother that people from all over India used to see him and were healed of cancer, and even snake bite. He was a man of great humility who lived with simplicity, not in a Bishop's palace adorned in regalia, but in a simple white gown in a hut amongst the people of his diocese, and he was greatly loved by all the people.

The Station Angel

Peter was keen on a girl whose father was a judge and a QC. They had been visiting friends some way from London and he had run out of money for the train fare back. He was always rather spend-thrift in his youth. The girl did not have money on her – after all, she wasn't expecting to be escorted by such an impecunious gentleman. Peter was at a loss as to what to do when a person (the station angel), overhearing him in his embarrassment, gave him the money for his fare and said, "You have an honest face, young man, I know you'll send it back when you can" and then disappeared after exchanging addresses. His copybook was not blotted and he was able to get the girl back to her home before incurring the wrath of the law! The kind 'angel' was also repaid.

Angels in France

Peter and his friend Wim, rather naïve old Stonyhurst boys, decided that they should have a weekend in Paris as part of their education! Both, we are told, were somewhat 'green about the gills' and on the loose in 'sin city'! The first night they decided to go to a bar that had soft lights and elegant furnishings. A beautiful girl joined them at the bar. After polite conversation Peter was told he could have her for nothing as he had such beautiful Irish eyes. They beat a hasty retreat when they realised they were in a high class brothel! Another occurrence was in a nightclub when two girls joined them. One said she was going to strip for Wim, which she did. They rejoined the table and Peter enquired why the other did not follow suit; he asked what she was prepared to do for him and after a meaningful glance to her friend she then said "I will dance for you." Sensing something was not as it appeared to be, and with youthful curiosity, he passed his hand over her lap to discover to his horror that the luxurious looking lady was in fact a man. Peter and Wim headed out of the establishment at great speed. WHAT IN THE WORLD DO YOU THINK THIS HAS TO DO WITH ANGELS? Read on, my friend…

Following this incident they were going down the Champs-Elysées in Wim's sports car, both wearing their 'old school ties', which happened to bear the cross of St. Omer, which resembles the Cross of Lorraine, which was, of course, the de Gaulle symbol. At the time there were riots in Paris between the Gaullists and the Communists and they were being swept along on a tide of cheering Gaullists crying, "Vive de Gaulle!" when suddenly the on-coming Communists, seeing the two innocents abroad wearing their old school ties, started to hurl chairs over the bonnet and rock the car. The pair escaped at great speed down a side street, the car somewhat battered, but both boys intact.

As a result their slim funds were somewhat depleted so they decided to head back to Calais and the UK. However, on arrival at the port they found the ferry had been cancelled and they would have to go to Dunkirk. The petrol tank was almost empty and they had eaten the last of the rolls that the kindly hotel proprietor had given them on leaving Paris, when they spotted a little café. Wim had a few Dutch guilders and successfully exchanged them for francs. Having bought some petrol, they went into the café and were contemplating whether they should buy some food with their remaining money or ring Peter's fiancée in England, who might have become worried. However, the barman at this point, having indicated that he spoke no English, leaned across and said, "Monsieur, don't waste your money – love is like the Camembert – it don't last!!" However, the Frenchman was proved wrong: Peter was happily married for thirty-two years.

You may well say…"I don't see many angels in this saga", but that is still to come……

Having eaten their last morsels and limped into Dunkirk with a practically empty tank, they approached the totally deserted dock. Wim wisely had bought a return ticket, but Peter hadn't and he was wondering how on earth he was going to pay for the ferry! Then in the mists of the early morning, two figures emerged out the haze… Peter exclaimed to his friend "I know these people." By this time Wim's humour was wearing a little thin… "Oh come on, I've had enough of your optimism"…but it was true, they were acquaintances Peter knew from India. They greeted him warmly and within minutes Peter was asking them to lend him some money, which they gladly did (although, typically, Peter had no cheque book with him and his friend had to give them a cheque on his behalf!)

DON'T YOU SEE, THESE TWO, SWIRLING OUT FROM THE MURK OF THE DOCK IN THE NICK OF TIME, CERTAINLY PROVED TO BE ANGELS!!

A postscript to this little story: once on board, they headed for the bar and a slap-up meal, when a reporter happened to over-hear them talking and asked for their story. Some weeks later Peter received a call from a friend who worked in the French Embassy saying, "Wow, you could have started an incident with your escapade with the ex-Communists in France." The article had appeared in the French Press! It was later to appear in the *Daily Mail* with a footnote saying, "When Englishmen go to Paris it is not advisable for them to wear their old school ties." (They certainly wouldn't do so in this day and age!)

It seemed that Peter had been rescued once before; the angels appeared to feel he was worth protecting.

Swiss Angel

Peter and Mavis were returning from India on home leave as Peter was working out there. They boarded a Swissair plane in Bombay, but it only took them to Switzerland, then they had to change airlines to fly to the UK.

Unfortunately Peter had picked up some sort of stomach bug and spent most of the flight in the toilet. Mavis was left with three children aged five, three and one, two of whom proceeded to race up and down the plane, much to her embarrassment, and the staff did not seem to care!

Arriving in Zurich Peter headed for the Gents while Mavis attempted to tidy the children ready for their meeting with their grandparents when they got to the UK. Several years had passed since they had last seen each other and the grandparents had not yet met two of the children. Attempting to handle all three children, Mavis was distracted for a moment, in which the elder son, excited by seeing so many aeroplanes, managed to get out onto the runway. He was rescued by a young man, who escorted him swiftly back to his frantic mother!

Realising her difficulty he offered to look after the five and three year olds whilst she took the youngest to change her nappy and put her into warm clothes. Today one would be highly suspicious of such an offer, but to Mavis it was heaven sent! She accomplished her task and returned to find the two children being highly entertained by the courageous stranger! At that moment Peter appeared, poor man, still looking rather pale and exhausted, to find all the children looking immaculate and happy. Mavis, in all the confusion, suddenly realised that the kind stranger had disappeared before she had been able to thank him. SHE NEVER FORGOT THAT ANGEL!

The Angel in Egypt

Rosemary had gone to Egypt and was interested in tracing the journey of the Holy Family during their sojourn there. She had wanted, in particular, to see 'The Church of the Apparitions', where it had been reported that the Holy Family had appeared to Moslem and Christian alike, but she had been unable to find a map with the church on it.

Just as Rosemary and her husband were heading for the airport she noticed a half drawn map on the wall of the hotel where they had spent the night, and noticed that the church was shown on it and was on their route to the airport. As they had an hour to spare she begged her reluctant husband to agree to visit it, and though he said they might miss their plane, finally, after much discussion, they boarded the train. However, they went a stop too far, and her husband pleaded with her not to proceed. She insisted they should alight and retrace their journey to the previous stop. At this moment a man in the uniform of the Egyptian army appeared. He had overheard them discussing their dilemma. He beamed. "I am a Christian, I will show you the way" and insisted on escorting them himself.

Whilst in the train he was saying how pleased he was to meet some Christians from the west. He explained it was difficult to follow Christianity in a country where it was a minority religion. He said he had attended Mass that morning, but had not been to communion and somehow he felt meeting them was a message from God. He took them to the church and then to the basilica afterwards, where Mass was in progress. Rosemary thanked him profusely, told how he was truly a messenger from heaven and left him to receive holy communion.

Rosemary was thrilled with all she saw, but by this time her husband was urging her to hurry as the plane would go without them. "No," she replied, "God brought us here and He will make sure the plane will still be there on our arrival!" She was right!

Angel of Letters

Visiting the post office to buy stamps was not something Sharon did very often and really didn't like writing letters much. Since the birth of the internet she was very happy that most correspondence could now be done without using stamps. However, when it came to birthdays and friends who still had not caught up with the twentieth century, stamps were occasionally required.

It was one of those days to visit the post office. So, feeling pleased with herself for actually getting it together to buy and write birthday cards, Sharon left her office to walk to the local post office. To do this she had to cross two main roads. The first and most busy was negotiated with ease because there were traffic lights and pedestrian crossings. She came to the second set of lights to cross the road to the post office. There she stood waiting for the green man to indicate it was safe to walk and for the lights to go red for the cars. There was no one with her and her thoughts wandered to things that were going on at work.

Then the lights changed. As they did, the letters she had in her hand just suddenly *left* her hand. She cannot remember or understand why she let go of them, but as she reached down to pick them up, a voice in her head said there was a good reason for the letters falling to the ground. It was like slow motion – as her hand finally found the letters on the ground, a car ran the red light at high speed, passing straight in front of her. It all happened so fast, but Sharon knew that if she had not dropped the letters and reached down to pick them up, she would have walked straight into the path of the car and at the speed it was travelling she would have been killed instantly.

Sharon was completely shaken by this but realised something amazing had just happened; an angel had been with her. She knew for certain that it had made sure she dropped the letters to save her life. Her shock turned to joy; it made her feel more alive than ever before and she thanked her Angel of Letters that day, telling all in the office about what had just occurred.

An Angel in Cairo

Sharon and her Irish friend Gillian, both in their early twenties, back in 1988, decided that they would get away from the rat race in London and visit Australia, but booked to visit Egypt, starting with Cairo, en route.

They felt it was an intrepid journey into the unknown but with the optimism of youth felt nothing could go wrong.

On a fresh, English spring evening Gillian and Sharon boarded a plane destined for Cairo, Egypt, a city that held the mystery and energy of the magnificent Egyptian ancient dynasty and the great pyramids.

They were excited, but ignorant of what lay before them. They had been advised by a friend, Nick, that the best place to find accommodation was in Talet Harb Street in the 'main drag' of Cairo and there they should look for a place called the Oxford Pension. Nick had said that this place, though basic, was clean and cheap.

They thought that it would be easy, just hail a cab and tell the driver to go there. How wrong could they be?

Arriving at 11.00 p.m. Cairo time, they were immersed into the Arabic hubbub and confusion. Immediately on arrival their passports were seized, plus their luggage. Bewildered, they asked the Customs officers what they were doing. Grins and nods were their only answer.

Eventually their passports and luggage emerged and they

headed off to the taxi ranks. They were greeted by a flood of long robed, scruffy taxi drivers with equally scruffy, dented cars.

"A car, Madam," said one with a toothless grin and very untrustworthy eyes. "No thanks," they thought. Sharon asked another if he knew the Oxford Pension.

"Oh yes, but full, Madam." She did not believe him. He then telephoned someone, with whom she spoke and he confirmed this. She rather naïvely believed him! "I have a friend who has a hotel," the driver said, "– I take you, yes?"

Tired and exasperated by this time, they agreed. They were whisked off at breakneck speed through the city of Cairo and seemed to keep going.

Luckily Sharon asked about certain landmarks, identifying the Ramsey station, in the heart of Cairo and had some idea of their bearings. After that it became a blur.

The heat and dust were already penetrating their weary bodies and the various aromas of spices were at times intoxicating. All they could think was of a bed to lay their heads. Finally they reached the elusive Talet Harb Street after what seemed an endless journey.

After paying the driver the equivalent of £25 in Egyptian money they realised they had been ripped off, just as Jack had warned them. This was not Talet Harb, but fatigue had the better of them.

They had arrived outside a hotel which, from the outside, looked fairly respectable. When they were shown their room, on drawing back the sheets of the double bed, it was clear that perhaps an 'Achmed' and his harem had spent several sweaty nights no doubt consummating their love. They were totally overwhelmed! Fortunately they had been given a clean sheet for the other bed and Sharon had a spare sheet with her. So they stripped 'Achmed's' soiled shrouds and donned their own.

The night was a scratchy one as the bed bugs found new flesh to feed on! A few swiftly downed Jameson drams helped them get through the night!

Dawn saw them beat a hasty retreat from the inaptly named 'Hotel del Rosa' to find the real Talet Harb Street. They hopped into another taxi for a somewhat chaotic ride, the driver picking up a motley crew of 'cousins' jabbering away in Arabic and ignoring them completely! They were swiftly learning facts about how the Egyptians operated, but had not worked out a strategy as to how to deal with them. Their first prerogative was to reach Talet Harb.

After almost two hours they finally arrived at their destination. However, they were stymied once more by their inability to read the street or hotel signs. Slight panic and frustration started to rock their confidence.

Somehow they managed to find the Egyptian tourist board. They climbed up four flights of dusty old Victorian stairs and saw two rooms, which had once been beautifully furnished but everything had reached a state of dilapidation. There were several old men smoking shisha (the local tobacco). No help was offered. No one had heard of the Oxford Pension. No one had a map.

They then thought the next place to go was a posh hotel, so after wandering about they found the Hilton Hotel, where they had a drink as they were convinced a staff member would be able to help them. No one could, and even the hotel did not have a map!

By this time they had almost given up, having been pushed from pillar to post, misled and ripped off; they were still determined to enjoy themselves, but were certainly not achieving that goal.

Finally Sharon suggested that they go to the British Embassy, where she thought they would at least be able to get a city map in English. She was feeling optimistic and told Gillian to have some faith, something would happen. So with new hope in their hearts they headed off to the Embassy, which they managed to find reasonably easily, which Sharon took as a good sign.

However, on arrival the news was not so good – the Embassy was shut. By now it was about 2 p.m. and the heat was high. Sharon and Gillian were starting to get very worried about their belongings, locked in the dodgy Hotel Rosa. Gillian was not impressed and Sharon asked if she had any other ideas. She hadn't. Sharon said she just had a feeling help would come and they should wait. So they did. The time ticked away…2.30 p.m., 3 p.m.…it was getting later and hotter. By around 3.30 p.m. both were exasperated…what were they to do! Sharon said again, "Look, we just have to wait, something will happen." Just as she said this it did.

They had both had their eyes trained on one particular spot

most of the time – they were outside the front of the Embassy but had continued to look at the corner to its right. Then they arrived. Coming around that corner was a tall, dark haired man, dressed in black, with a young blond man, whose hair shone like gold. Sharon screamed "Look!" to Gillian and both girls started running towards the two men – the first Europeans they had seen all day as well.

As they got closer they realised the man in black was in fact a priest and the blond man a lad of about seventeen. The both started talking at once and they discovered the priest was from where Gillian lived, Belfast, and the young man – called Richard – said his father worked at the embassy and he was on school holidays.

Gillian and Sharon breathlessly rattled off their story so fast that Richard held up his hand to stop them in their tracks and suggested they go for a coffee, sit down quietly and sort things out. Sharon was very impressed with this calm approach from such a youth. So they did, they sat down and talked; Richard then helped them find the Oxford Pension, but it was full so they found another, much grander sounding, place called The Clarage – which had been an amazing hotel in its heyday. However run down the premises, the staff were friendly and they were now in the more 'happening' part of the city.

Finding the Hotel del Rosa again was not so easy but the angelic Richard was patient and stayed with them talking Arabic to the driver and taking charge of these rather panicked twenty-plus year olds. Finally they found their belongings and got back to the Clarage. They had a well earned drink and a meal. It was the start of a wonderful five days, in which Richard was their guide and friend, showing them Cairo in a way that no tour guide ever could. He was a true angel and saved the day.

RICHARD, TO THE TWO GIRLS, WITH HIS TALL, ERECT POSTURE, GOOD LOOKS AND GENTLE MANNER, WAS CERTAINLY THEIR ANGEL AND HAD THEIR EVERLASTING GRATITUDE!

The Comforting Angel

June found her way to the Jack and Jill windmills overlooking the village of Ditchling in Sussex. She had her dog, Simba, with her, who loved that particular walk. It was a beautiful day and the view was breathtaking.

However, she found herself in tears, realising that she may not see this wonderful sight again, as she had been diagnosed with terminal cancer by her doctor that week. She realised how much she would miss her friends and family and had needed to get away from them all, so as not to depress them with her deep sadness.

Suddenly a middle aged lady walked up and asked if she could share her bench. They found themselves talking as if they were old friends and she revealed her recently acquired knowledge to the person.

It is strange how sometimes you meet someone for the first time and immediately you find they are absolutely on your wavelength. They discussed politics, families, world problems, and finally June found herself talking about her church and her community and said how much it meant to her. Her friend said, "Well that is really a good thing, as you will need them." She continued, "However, you have no need to worry, you will make a full recovery."

At that moment Simba distracted June and she walked up to where he was to see what he was doing. Once she found out he was merely burrowing down a rabbit hole with great excitement, she turned back to her new friend. SHE HAD COMPLETELY VANISHED!

June went on to make a full recovery and though she revisited the spot she never saw the lady again.

Airport Angels

After Peter left India, nearing the end of the 1960s, he found a job with an American company whose UK subsidiary was based in London. He had recently been promoted to Managing Director for the UK and he had been asked to go to Boston to meet the President of the company and all the executives for the first time.

At Heathrow he went to the departure desk and was asked, "Where is your visa?" He had asked his secretary to book the flight and having been back and forth to India and the UK when a visa was not required at that time, he was completely shocked. He was told that he could not board the aircraft. He then asked the clerk at the counter to call her boss. He finally appeared and Peter explained that he had to be in Boston by the next day and told him the importance of his visit. The man said, "But, sir, you will have to go back to the US embassy." Peter said, "There is a procession going on in the centre of London today, there is no way I can get there and back in time to get a flight for my meeting. Is there no other way?" The man thought for a while and then came up with the idea that he could book him on a flight from Boston to Canada and said that he could tell Border Control in Boston that he was 'in transit'. "Wonderful," said Peter. "Do that. You are a good man."

When Peter arrived in Boston the President of the company was astonished when he heard his story. "I have never heard of anyone being allowed into the USA without a visa!" Peter went up in his estimation as someone who could use his initiative so brilliantly!

PETER, HOWEVER, ATTRIBUTED THIS TO THE ANGEL WHO HAD RESCUED HIM BACK AT HEATHROW!

To end the story, he duly returned via Canada, and some weeks later Mavis received a phone call one evening from the Foreign Office, saying, "We have a record that your husband left the country for the USA but we have no record of his return." Mavis assured them that he was back and had returned via Canada! She believed that as he had an Irish surname (due to the troubles at that time) they had followed his every move over all the journeys he had made.

The Dorchester Angel

For sixteen years before his death Peter had had leukaemia, but since the first year when Mavis, his wife, suggested he go to Lourdes, apart from medication, he had kept remarkably well and active. However, they had not had a holiday in years; with the vagaries of bringing up a family, school fees etc., holidays took a very low priority. On this occasion, however, they decided to take the holiday of a lifetime and go on a Caribbean cruise. This was not such a common occurrence as it is today.

On arriving at Heathrow by bus from Gatwick, they were checking in their luggage at the flight desk when they realised that the vanity case was missing. Apart from Mavis's cosmetics it contained the all-important pills for Peter's well-being. Visions of rushing to doctors in a foreign country and trying to get a prescription entered their minds and their spirits sank.

"It must be in the back of the bus," said Peter. "Say a prayer and I'll get it back, you continue queuing."

He rushed out of the terminal to hail a taxi, but the taxi declined such a spuriously unprofitable fare. At this point a concierge in full Dorchester Hotel uniform appeared. He had been listening to the conversation Peter had had with the taxi driver. "Don't worry," he said, "see this car here, they are plain clothed policemen, they'll take you to wherever you want." "Yes, sir," replied the occupants, "jump in, we'll help you."

They sped around the airport complex in search of the bus. Peter saw it parked and they found the driver having a cup of tea. He opened up the luggage compartment and sure enough the vanity case was there!

Meanwhile, Mavis had reached the top of the queue and was explaining the problem to the check-in clerk, who seemed mildly irritated and said, "Are you getting on this flight or not?" "Yes, we certainly are," Mavis replied with total confidence. She recalled a friend's last words: "I will pray you have a trouble free journey." At that moment Peter appeared triumphantly flourishing the vanity case.

They were confident their prayers would be answered but had never dreamt it would come about in the form of a Dorchester concierge...! Come to think of it, have you ever seen one at Heathrow?

They never saw another!

More Airport Angels

In the late 1960s Peter had an important business engagement in Holland. Mavis was going to drop him at Gatwick airport in West Sussex. In those days Gatwick had very few flights and not the great terminals it has today.

There had been torrential rain all night, but things appeared to be all right around the house, although that morning on the radio they heard that there had been severe flooding. They thought it was the media exaggerating, as they are prone to do.

They drove along without any apparent problems, when they found the road ahead was flooding rapidly and decided to seek another route. Five minutes later that road was closed so they decided to try the back road to the airport. A fire engine and fire tender were there pumping out a ditch.

Peter set out with his briefcase, bowler hat and city pinstriped suit and asked them if they would take him to the terminal. They said they weren't able to do that, but the fire tender was going to the runway area and the driver said, "Jump in." Another man, who had also abandoned his car, but had wisely donned Welling-ton boots, also decided to hitch a ride.

They set off, with the driver saying, "Watch out for any planes landing!" They got within about a hundred yards of the terminal when a huge puddle made their passage further impossible.

The man in his gumboots set off, but the driver of the tender stopped him. "Give this fellow a piggy back" – indicating Peter. The man looked slightly taken aback, but before he knew it Peter had leapt on his back. However, Peter's weight proved too much and he felt himself slipping. Just at that moment the tender driver, who had been watching this extraordinary sight, marched through the flood, grabbed Peter and put him astride his back like a Colossus, with Peter's shoes just half an inch above the offending water, and with a grin deposited Peter on the steps to the terminal.

All this was witnessed by cheering passengers watching from above! Peter arrived without even getting his feet wet! Peter said, "I can't thank you enough" and whipped a note into his hand. "I can't take that, sir – it was a pleasure!" said the driver. "I insist," said Peter. "If it makes you feel any happier I will charge it as transport to my company." Reluctantly the 'angel' then accepted the proffered note! What would Peter have done without him!

This story does not end here. Peter found on arrival at Gatwick that all the planes had been cancelled and there were hardly any trains. He waited around on the platform for a train for several hours when suddenly a train pulled in. It was going directly to Bognor Regis and stopping only at Horsham.

Peter decided this was not good enough in the circumstances and went to talk to the driver, who said, "Instructions are instructions."

By this time an eager crowd had gathered and were all clambering round requesting that the train should stop at Ifield, Crawley, Faygate and all manner of other stops. Peter pleaded with the man, but he was adamant. Then Peter said, "If we pulled the communication cord you would have to stop, wouldn't you?" "Yes," the besieged driver replied. "Well, we would have to pay the fine then, wouldn't we?" Peter retorted. By this time the considerably increased crowd had gathered, so Peter turned to them and questioned, "You'll all help to pay the fine won't you?" "Yes," they all chorused, "we'll all chip in."

The train driver and guard realised they were beaten and the train proceeded with the promise of stops all along the way! Although Peter was not able to leave for Holland that day, he finally arrived home about 10 p.m.

Undaunted, he set off to Heathrow the next day. He was so delighted to have actually achieved this and was busy phoning home to say he had arrived at the airport, when he heard them calling his flight. After dashing down the endless corridors to the departure gate, he found to his dismay that all the passengers had caught the bus to take them to the aircraft, and had gone.

Undaunted, he ventured gingerly onto the runway and hailed a passing car. Its occupant was an Alitalia pilot and Peter asked him to find his plane!! "Certainly, sir" and sped off circling the various planes on the tarmac until he found it! Peter was then dropped on the tarmac VIP style at the foot of the gangway. "Bless you, my friend, I may not see you again in this life, but I'll definitely see you in heaven," gasped Peter as the Alitalia 'angel' grinned and sped off on his interrupted journey.

With security as it is today, this would be an impossibility!

TWO ANGELS FOR THE BUSINESS TRIP, which, despite the difficulties, actually ended very successfully!!

The Child Angel

It had been a particularly bad week; the pain of losing Peter, who had died of leukaemia aged 59 when he had so much to give to the world, had been very great. Mavis felt no one understood. People had been demanding of her, perhaps lacking sensitivity and saying trivial things – "At least you are financially OK." Little did they know how little money mattered at that moment to her and that she would rather be penniless and have him back. She was tired and felt alone and abandoned by God and felt the presence of her husband's spirit fading, which previously she had felt so close.

She attended Mass at the Church of our Lady of Consolation at West Grinstead. This is a church with a great history as the main house has a priest hole and during the Reformation the Caryll family sheltered the priest who was later martyred. It is now a place of pilgrimage. Situated in the countryside it serves several of the surrounding villages.

It was always a source of solace and she attended as usual. She came out of Mass and was talking to one of their friends, David. He said, "I must tell you what Georgie [his little girl of about eight or nine] said." Georgie had two sisters who were very keen horse-women, and because of Peter's love of the equestrian sport they loved to share their experiences with him. However, Georgie had been too young to ride whilst he was alive, but had remembered the long exchanges her sister had had with Peter. Georgie's grandfather was very ill and they had prepared her with the fact that he may die. Her father was going to see him after Mass. Before he had left home Georgie had come up to him and said, "Please tell Grandpa that when he gets to heaven to tell him to say to Peter that I am now riding!"

The positive faith of that small child is indeed a very great lesson to us, that death is not to be feared and the certainty that 'those who live in the Lord will never see each other for the last time'. She was certainly a little angel to Mavis that day – she left the church hugely uplifted.

Angel at the Convent

Peter's daughters had attended a well known convent school in Sussex. They had been very happy there and had made their mark with their singing, piano playing and sport. Peter had always been a vociferous voice encouraging the girls in their various netball matches etc. and the family built up a good relationship with the nuns.

The head teacher was a nun at the time. On the day of Peter's death, she was in her room when an intruder broke in and attacked her. Somehow, although she was slight in build, in her terror she felt the most enormous strength and managed to fight him off and he disappeared through the window.

When she heard that Peter had died that day, she attributed her defeat of the intruder to his help in summoning her Guardian Angel to protect her!

Angels in Greece

Mike and Mavis boarded a bus to the far end of the island of Skopelos in the Aegean sea, and were entertained all the way by the singing bus conductor (they found out later that he actually owned all the buses)!!

At the end of the journey they joined him for a coffee and his friend came and sat at the table. They were not sure what their programme was once they had arrived at their destination, but the friend urged them to visit the church of St. John. He said it was the most holy of places and when he had worked in Australia he had thought of it many times and it had remained his ambition to visit it again when he finally retired to his beloved island of Skopelos! (This church is actually depicted in the film 'Mamma Mia', but the film had not been made at that time.)

Mike and Mavis set off on foot along the coastline, enjoying the wonderful scenery and the scent of pines and herbs, and passing some strange scarecrow-like figures high on a rock. They later found out that the locals change the clothes on the figures frequently!

They did not pass a single car or person on their journey and after at least an hour's walk were enchanted with the monastery up circa 300 steps, whence the views were breathtaking. They were trying to picture how the monks would have lived years ago in such a remote area.

Afterwards they ate their picnic on the tiny stony beach and swam in the warm crystal clear sea.

So idyllic were their surroundings they were startled to see that time had passed by so quickly that there was no hope of catching the last bus. They started to retrace their steps to the small town where the bus had brought them, thinking they would have to find somewhere to stay for the night. Suddenly from out of the blue a jeep drew up. Two young English people hailed them: "You must be English", quoting "Mad dogs and Englishmen go out in the midday sun." They heard about Mike and Mavis's problem and offered them a lift back to Skopelos town.

Remember the fact that Mike and Mavis had not seen a soul all day!! TWO ENGLISH ANGELS ON A GREEK ISLAND!!

On Another Greek Island

Mike and Mavis were on their honeymoon (both nearing retirement) on the picturesque island of Samos, also in the Aegean sea, not far from the coast of Turkey. They decided to take a boat trip round the island and set off admiring the wonderful scenery and the Captain's hospitality with ouzo and mezes!! Halfway around they paused at a remote harbour and decided to go to the nearest beach and taverna and thoroughly enjoyed the unique natural setting amongst the olive trees and vines, where they were welcomed in the true Greek style with great hospitality and kindness.

They were due to be back at the harbour at 2.15 p.m. At about 1.55 they set off, but had forgotten there was a steep hill ahead (coming down had taken no time) and now, panting and racing as fast as they could, they reached the summit to find the boat leaving the harbour! Despite their wild gesticulations and shouts it disappeared round the headland! No headcount had been taken!

As it was siesta time in Greece the tiny harbour was totally deserted. They set off to find some sort of town, having no idea in which direction they should be heading. A little girl tending sheep appeared who was unable to help them, not understanding their faltering Greek and very concerned about her flock. They were poorly equipped, wearing flip flops and swimming gear and with scarcely any money, most of it having been spent in the taverna!

Eventually, after trudging under the boiling sun, they found a small village taverna firmly closed with not a soul in sight! They sat under a welcoming tree wondering what they could possibly do. It happened there was a bus stop opposite but with no notice of bus times or any other information.

Eventually an old woman appeared from nowhere and they managed to ask her when the next bus to Samos town was due. She had a little English and said there was a bus but it only ran one day a week, but it happened to be today! They waited with her and after some time a bus appeared and they were prepared to board it. But the woman said no, she was going on it, but their bus to Samos was due in ten minutes. What a relief – it came, as she had said; they eagerly boarded the bus and found they had just enough money to pay the fare! WHAT AN ANGEL SHE WAS!

Rupert Brooke's Greek Angel

Mike and Mavis decided to visit the Greek island of Skyros whilst they were staying on Skopelos. They boarded a 'flying dolphin' hovercraft, arriving in the afternoon.

They booked into a hotel that was just built, some of the rooms being not quite ready. The main reason for their visit was to see the grave of Rupert Brooke, the poet who had died of septicaemia on a naval vessel, Skyros having been the nearest island on which to bury him.

However, when they arrived they found there were no buses going out there, they had not brought their driving licences with them and there seemed to be no way of going there as it was at the other end of the island.

In the courtyard there appeared a gentleman, whom Mike took to be the owner, who introduced himself. They immediately engaged in earnest conversation. Mike told him the reason for their coming to Skyros and after much discussion about Greek mythology and other topics, the man introduced himself as George. Mike told him about their wish to see Rupert Brooke's grave and the difficulties they were having getting there. George replied, "He is my hero" and went on to say, "If you are ready at 7 a.m. tomorrow I will take you there myself."

Next morning, true to his word, his car was awaiting them promptly and they sped off on what proved to be a fascinating journey. George was a fount of knowledge with a deep love of his island. He pointed out the beach where he said Achilles dressed up as woman to avoid the call up of the Trojan war!

The terrain was fairly barren with outcrops of rocks and curiously square topped bushes on which numerous goats stood, using them as vantage points. George said that every goat on the island was unique, no two looked the same, and indeed it seemed that was so when Mike and Mavis observed them carefully! He also pointed out that he knew his own goats by the tag on their ear.

As they approached the site there were hundreds of rocks all painted in various colours with hieroglyphics all over them. He pointed out that they had significance, yellow for jealousy, red for love etc., and they listened with fascination. The island is well known for its spiritual quality and there are many visitors seeking the alternative way of life.

The actual grave of Rupert Brooke was so startling it took their breath away! Amid this barren terrain appeared a delightful olive grove. The tomb itself looked exactly as one which would appear in any English graveyard, with his famous poem *The Soldier* etched on each side in both English and Greek.

Mike read out the poem and the lines 'If I should die, think only this of me: That there's some corner of a foreign field that is for ever England' and the final verse, 'And think, this heart, all evil shed away, A pulse in the eternal mind, no less Gives somewhere back the thoughts by England given; Her sights and sounds; dreams happy as her day; And laughter, learnt of friends; and gentleness, in hearts at peace, under an English heaven.'

How strange that he should write this, with obviously some premonition in his mind, and it sent shivers down their spines and brought tears to their eyes.

They returned to Samos and George invited them for coffee to some apartments he owned. Mike continued his conversation about the history of the island, which proved extremely interesting. Mike asked George where he had been during the war and he said he was in Skyros. Mike asked him what year he was born. "1944," he replied. "Well, that's a coincidence," said Mike, "I was born in 1944; what month?" George replied, "August." "So was I," replied Mike, with increasing astonishment. "What day?"

"The eighth," retorted George. "I can't believe it," Mike replied excitedly. "I have never met anyone born on the same day as me."

NOT ONLY DID GEORGE PROVE TO BE THEIR ANGEL, BUT WAS ALMOST LIKE A TWIN TO MIKE!

Greek Taxi Driver Angel

A Dutch lady was visiting the island of Karpathos, an unspoilt island in the Dodecanese, and became extremely ill. A taxi was called to take her to the airport to fly to Rhodes for treatment. On arrival at the airport the woman found that in her panic and pain she had left her money behind. The taxi driver said, "Don't worry, Madam, you can pay me when you return"! "However," he said, "you will need some money in Rhodes to get to the hospital" and he handed her 100 euros!

WHAT AN ANGEL HE WAS!!

Angel in a Glass!

Helen was feeling depressed and anxious as her son, far away in Japan, had leukaemia. He had been in a 'bubble' for months to keep him from infection but today he was having a life saving bone marrow transplant and she was praying hard in her kitchen. She picked up her favourite glass, which she had kept for years in the kitchen to take a drink of water, when she noticed it had a deep crack in it. Quite irrationally she felt overwhelmed with tears over such a small occurrence. She asked her husband whether he had cracked it and he denied it, saying he never used it.

Next morning she went to get the glass to wrap it up safely for disposal when she noticed to her astonishment that the crack had gone! She called out to her husband, who was equally surprised.

Suddenly a feeling of great relief and intense warmth and comfort overwhelmed her. She cried out, "It is a sign from my Guardian Angel I Sean will come through this well and will be all right."

To this day, though tired, he is making good progress.

Miss Tiggie Cat Angel

"NOW," YOU WILL SAY, "SHE IS GOING TOO FAR, SHE MUST BE DERANGED."

We built a property on a Greek island in 2005. Greece is well known for its feral cats, and of course they scrounged food from us, but never dared venture near us. However, the year of my seventieth birthday, a beautiful cat wearing a collar strolled in, lay on the kitchen floor, walked from room to room and decided to stay! Later on she arrived with four kittens and hid them in the wall in the garden, so of course they had to be fed, but she refused them entry to the house at all times! Since then we have had her spayed as we felt she was being weakened by the continual births of kittens. When it comes to our leaving to return to the UK we feel heartbroken. However, we realised she belonged to someone else and would probably go back to them, which she did in our absence.

Ever since (now six years on) a couple of days after we return (which is twice a year) she again takes up residence. We call her Miss Tiggie and she answers to that, but no doubt has a Greek name too! We have established she belongs to an old lady in the village, who knows where she is but apparently does not object!! For Miss Tiggie to go back to the village, she must undertake a sheer rock climb of about 500 feet above us.

Each time we are nervous that she may no longer be with us, as we do not know her age, but every time she appears she is greeted with such excitement and delight, which is reciprocated when she rushes in to rekindle our love.

41

We have always had cats and dogs, but with going abroad so much we are unable to entertain the idea of having one in the UK. However, we feel our home is complete with Miss Tiggie and therefore to us SHE IS DEFINITELY AN ANGEL!

Author's Note

The first part of this book comprises real stories from people I have known, but I sometimes get the urge to write poetry. I cannot do it to order, but when the feeling comes on me, it seems to me that my Guardian Angel takes over and I barely change words I pen. I am told by authorities on the subject of angels that my birth sign indicates that Archangel Raphael is the angel allocated to me, who is apparently the angel of creativity, so I am merely the messenger!

The Christian

We say that we are Christians,
That means to follow Him,
Is that what you and I do
Or is our light still dim?

He gave us one commandment,
Which sums up all the rest,
It's simply, "Love your neighbour",
Just give yourself the test.

Do you fight your family
Or those with whom you work?
For the old, the sick, the ugly,
Does distaste inside you lurk?

There'd be no wars, no violence,
Divorce, no strikes, no strife,
If all obeyed that rule
We'd have a fine new life.

The answer's very simple,
Before you take a pace
Just say – "Would Christ do that
If he were in my place?"!

His power lies deep within us,
Just open up the door,
Let it flow right through you
You'll feel it strong and sure.

So be a good example,
Let joy be in your face
Then all the non-believers
Will want to know God's Grace

Christmas Eve

Cupboard stuffed to overflowing
Fridges bulging at the seams,
Spicy, pine-scented air, logs a'glowing
Crackling paper, sparkling tinsel, cloistered whispering, hissing
irons.

Glistening lights on glittering trees,
Weariness expunged by gutted anticipation, is all that's done that
had to be? Checking lists, steaming pans, endless topping
mounds of Brussels, stuffing birds, clove studded pinkened hams
waiting tantalising there.

Cats with slavering jaws guard the door where turkey lies
Willing it to open and reward them with the prize!
Beds erected in odd corners, mounds of blankets, sheets and
towels
Waiting for the coming crowd.

Scarlet tablecloth, blood red candles, holly, mistletoe and ivy,
cards suspended. Father Christmas in the chimney, mince pie
and tipple awaits him there.
Warming whisky heats the edges of the slightly fraying nerves.
Piling into boots and over-garments, squeezing into several cars.
Frost a glistening on the road edge, jagged trees unbared, bizarre.

High steeples jutting jet ward, gentle tolling of the bells.
Suddenly the pace has slackened, a warming glow lies within.
Candles halo softened faces, the organ music swells the hearts
and the familiar carols dissolve all pain, As goodness rises in each
family for a precious moment, oh that it would never wane.

All at once the bells are ringing, children dance along the aisle,
bearing aloft the Baby Jesus for all to see and loud acclaim.
Gently He's laid in the manger, the lights blaze out, the Lord is
here, all the weariness falls away.
For this at last is Christ's Birth Day.

Give Christmas
to the Children

For us the Christmas season is a time of real re-birth
The memories still untainted, despite the woes of earth.
At Mass the Christmas story unfolds as if anew
Singing joyful carols midst pungent pine and yew.

Joyful family gatherings, turkey and mince pies
Exciting looking parcels, a feast for small round eyes.
Log fires and candles burning, lighting up the room
A warm and joyful haven, contrasting the media gloom.

We hear it all around us, people's gripes and moans
Shopping, cooking, shouting, a time of endless groans.
Stressed and tired their Christmas just becomes a bore
Drinking, eating, fighting – it's all another chore.

Our prayers are for the children, together let them find
A way to value Christmas with an unfettered mind
Parents please remind them of the joy of Christ's new birth,
Welcomed by hosts of angels when He visited our Earth.

Don't starve them of their dreams, give them what they need
Don't nourish them with media's answer of anger, lust and greed
Fill up their minds with goodness, lives full of love and sharing
So Christmas becomes a time for home, families and caring.

Put Christ Back Into Christmas

I went to buy a Christmas card
But found to my dismay
There were three religious pictures
Amongst hundreds on display!

The Hindus have Divali
The Muslims Ramadan
We Christians have lost our Christmas
On Our Lord there is a ban

We've just let it happen
It's us who are to blame
Too busy, too distracted
Our Lord's name to acclaim

We've angered Him by our neglect
His temple's a market place
His scourge would be upon us
We're really in disgrace

What can we do to reverse the trend?
Bring happiness back to homes
Put Christ back into Christmas
Instead of building domes

Angels Come in Strange Disguises

The millennium year has long since passed
Anniversary of his birth
What have we done to mark this?
Of remembrance there's a dearth.

We need to be more active
Bring the world His powerful grace
We cannot keep Him to ourselves
Let others see His face!

The Christmas Story

Frozen and tired the young couple sought
Food, shelter and warmth, but it could not be bought
The Babe in her womb no longer could wait
He was born in the hay of humble estate.
AND……THE INN-KEEPER SAID "NO!"

Bedazzled and dazed the poor shepherds fell,
When the angel appeared, the good news to tell
They were to follow the star whilst the heavens did ring
To find their young Lord, their humble babe King.
THEY HEARD……THE INN-KEEPER HAD SAID "NO"

The three wise men had heard the good news
They studied astronomy and exchanged learned views,
They hurried, gift-laden, excited, entranced
And worshipped and glorified
their King as they glanced.
THEN……KING HEROD SAID, "NO"!

Today we're too busy
Our Christmas cards sent
To think of the power of this amazing event.
We're thinking of turkey, plum pudding and wine
To give that much thought to the Infant Divine.

SAD, ……AS OF OLD – WE'RE STILL SAYING "NO"!

Christmas Ponderings

We blame it all on someone else
The government is one,
BUT the government is elected
The deed is truly done!

We blame our environment,
We blame our basic roots
BUT mother and our father
Not all could bank at Coutts!

Whatever seem our problems
Someone else's are much worse
How often have we hungered
And truly died from thirst!

Why can't we be more simple
Why let others take the blame
WE sometimes bring it on us
In our individual shame

Christmas is to remind us
However bad we are
God's son was born to take it,
His sign was that great Star.

We have a new beginning
Just as that Babe was born
To show the world that Jesus
Brings life to the forlorn.

The Sins of the Fathers (Mothers) are Visited on the Sons (Daughters)?

Sunken eyes and swollen belly,
Dressed in rags with bowl out held,
Waiting for a grain of rice
Victim of men's greed and vice,
Did you reap what you did sow?
Did parents cause this life below?

Arthritic hands and watering eyes
Gazing out at Christmas trees
Not a friend or neighbour near
Filled with misery and fear,
Did you reap what you did sow?
Did your parents cause this life below?

Dweller in this cardboard city
Dazzled by the glittering stores
Lost, confused, all world defiant
Cynical but self reliant
Did you reap what you did sow?
Did your parents cause this life below?

Baby lying in a manger
Only wrapped in swaddling clothes,
Joy and happiness abound
Peace and glory all around

Did you reap what you did sow?
Did your parents cause this life below?

Through the life of that small Babe
Whatever life puts in your way,
There can still be life and hope
And with tragedies you will cope
Did you reap what you did sow?
Did parents cause this life below?

As Christmas comes around this year
Reflect and see what you can do
Can you help to make things better
By acts and deeds, donations, letter?
Shall you reap what you did sow?
Did parents cause this life below?

The Eyes

Mother in labour toiling with sweat,
The babe's screams rending the air,
The sound, then the stare, made her forget
Her son's eyes sparkled with life, what joy, what reward!

Weeks pass, with child at her breast
So special a moment their eyes connect
The eyes close tightly, a moment at rest
Open and smile, crinkling up at the sides.

The priest lights a candle, baptismal vows renewed
Symbol of Christ to guide though the years
Small eyes watch the flicker, with holiness imbued
Born yet again to the life in the spirits.

Years pass, the eyes burning and tired
From revising exams and passing tests.
The letter is opened to read what is said.
The eyes say it all, he's passed! What relief!

A young girl is passing, tossing her hair,
Hips gently swinging, lips in a pout
This time it's him who gives her a stare
Blood surges, heart leaps, eyes glint with desire.

Mavis Thompson

Years pass, he is summoned from work,
Wife's grasping his hand and crying in pain
He looks down and tears start to jerk
His son looks up, new eyes see the world.

Eyes simmer with passion, shut tight in pain
Clouding in anger, watering with joy
Seeing ugliness and beauty in sun and in rain.
A life of experience, the eyes speak it all.

Disease grasps the body, eyes cloud and upward turn
Lungs gasp for air, blood starts to chill
As spirit leaves Earth no more to return
the eyes gaze to heaven, with love they seem to burn.

Sorrowing eyes, copious tears, deep sadness unfurled
The widow is left, shattered, bereft
His eyes turning in destroyed all her world
But his last heavenward glance proved paradise awaited.

When pining her loss, like a limb torn apart
She remembered those eyes, glowing with fire,
And warmth entered her empty cold heart
Those who lived in the Lord would again be united.

Easter Thoughts
Forgiveness

"My God, Thou hast forsaken me," He cried
The thorns he wore pierced His head
His side ripped open, bled and bled
His clothes and dignity all stripped
His hands and side were crudely ripped
Despite the savage, searing pain
His cry to God was not in vain
He turned to men beside Him hung
Their arms outstretched, their spirits flung
"Forgive their sins"…and then He died.

Although this is a tale of pain
Because He spoke those words sublime
We know that when it is our time
The lives we lead are not in vain
Those who believe will rise again,
Gone all our guilt, our rage, our sadness
Our foolishness, our sins, our madness
For in our hearts…He's there to reign.

The Easter Story

Darkness, death and deep despair
Alas our Lord was no more there
Depleted, cheated they stood forlorn
The temple curtain ripped and torn

A shadowy figure appeared from the gloom
As they crouched beside the tomb
"I told you I would never leave,
So wipe your tears and do not grieve"

The lesson we never seem to learn
We forget His promise and inward turn
This Easter let us think again
Give Him our plans, our joys our pain

We have a solid path to tread
Many hearts around us dead
Bring them all the Easter Story
So they may see the Living Christ's Glory

Easter Sunday

Her beloved lay entombed in stone
She felt bereft and all alone
A soft voice whispered in her ear
A warm hand brushed away her tear.
"Oh Master how can this be
You're here standing in front of me?"
He smiled, "I told you I would never leave
But you my child did not believe."

Do you believe, my friends, this day
That Christ is here in all you say
In all decisions you have to make
In time of trouble when hearts do ache?

Remember those who've never heard
That treasured scripture, Christ's own word.
The only reason you are here
To spread the news both far and near.

May Easter mean that you have heard
The true meaning of that spoken word
Give others hope in their despair
Their Lord is here to heal their wounds
And bring salvation from their tombs
Beware of all you say and do
Then Christ can live and work through you.

Blessed Easter

Easter dawns, from darkened tomb in glory our Lord breaks out.
Once more He gives us hope to be renewed, to cast out doubt
Our Easter prayer today is to keep us always in his Light
Through joys, laughter, or in pain, forever in his caring sight.

Easter Renewal

Under a blanket of snow hidden activity is taking place
New shoots unfurl, a sticky bud prepares to bare its face

A hibernating squirrel stirs, shrunken stomach, hunger gnaws
Unearthing his hidden stores slavering lips and tearing claws.

The moorhens race at feverish pace, building a precarious nest
Eggs all laid, till beaks break through…taking a temporary rest.

Easter dawns, from darkened tomb in glory Our Lord breaks
outstretched
Once more He gives us a chance to be renewed to cast out doubt.
Each year we slip into the grime, new intentions cast aside
Forgiveness, His redeeming grace, even though we all backslide.

Our Easter prayer today is to keep us always in His Light
Through joys, laughter, or in pain, forever in His caring sight.

On the Death
of a Loved One
Do Not Grieve

Do not grieve too long for me
For I am always there
In all you do, I'm with you everywhere.
Carry on the tasks I left undone
Until your time has run
Spread the love I have for you
(like ripples on a pond)
To generations new.

Personal Reflections
by the Author
Butterfly Angels

My daughter Deborrah had a great fear of moths and once during Mass at West Grinstead, what appeared to be a moth flew at her, but before she yelled out, she realised, thankfully, that it was only a butterfly. I remember it was during the month of January, when butterflies are not normally seen and my husband Peter remarked, "It must be the Holy Spirit."

My first husband, Peter, died of leukaemia in 1990, but the Easter before he died the altar was dramatically decorated with an amazingly imaginative cascade of flowers depicting the shroud falling down from the cross, created by a parishioner, Frances. A single rose fell poignantly out of the arrangement during the Mass and at the time of the raising of the host a butterfly descended onto the altar and again my husband remarked upon it.

Shortly before he died a nun visited us and we had a very interesting weekend as she had worked in Africa and was an amazingly dedicated, but very matter of fact person who had witnessed many tragedies and worked most of her life amongst deprived people. We received a delightful card from her following her visit with the inscription, 'Those who live in the Lord never see each other for the last time' and it was decorated with butterflies. I used this card in the Order of Service for my husband's funeral service as I felt the words were so very poignant and beautiful. Later these were printed on the memorial cross erected in his memory. We never saw the nun again.

Before he died we were discussing death and he said, "I can't bear to think that you will be on your own when I die." I said, "I'll cope, but I don't want to think about it now, every day is precious to us." I added, "Please send me a sign when it happens so I know you are in heaven."

On Christmas night in 1989, Peter's last Christmas (as I said, I did not realise the significance of butterflies at that time), my next door neighbour Beryl gave me two huge brightly coloured butterflies with chocolate in the middle. I wore them as earrings all evening for a laugh. After his death, on another Christmas, my granddaughter Chantelle, aged under two, went straight to the tree and said, "Look, butterflies." That evening another little girl, aged six, came to the door with a card she had painted. It had two silver candles with golden wicks and she said, "But do you know what they mean?" and I said, "Yes, they are the light of Christ come to the world." She said, "Yes, that's right" – what an astonishing thing for a small child to say. She spotted the butterflies on the tree and immediately settled down to draw them. She came running to show me when she had finished and there was a panic later on in the evening when it was time to go as she couldn't find the drawing, which she obviously treasured.

Later, I was looking at a collage of photos I had done for the year 1989 and saw I was wearing a top which I purchased that year for the hunt ball that had a large golden sequin butterfly on it. He loved that outfit. This was long before our conversation about him giving me a sign.

After the trauma of losing someone, so much has to be done in the way of bureaucracy and arrangements that momentarily you have little time to grieve. Some months later I was feeling very sad, lonely and missing Peter a great deal and had been decorating the church at West Grinstead with flowers when I cried out, "If you're still with me, please let a butterfly appear." Nothing happened! Later on that evening I had some friends for dinner and as we were finishing our meal one exclaimed, "Look, there's a moth." "No," I cried, "it is a butterfly" and sure enough it was! That was in October.

I remembered that I had asked him to send me a sign and it filled me with warmth and contentment. (I had no idea at the time that in many countries butterflies signify the Holy Spirit or the presence of angels.) At his funeral and in the following months butterflies continued to float around the church at Mass. From then on butterflies have been appearing to me on many occasions.

Shortly after this I visited an elderly friend for the weekend. I wanted to go to church and there was one round the corner. It was a bitterly cold, wet night in November. I said to myself, "Wouldn't it be amazing if a butterfly should appear here." Just when I was saying, "Mavis, donon'be an idiot, you're asking for the impossible", suddenly I saw the woman in front of me waving away something fluttering around her, and lo and behold it was another red admiral, which settled on my pew in front of me! What joy it gave me!

I later repeated this story to friends in the church and during the Mass I attended before I left for a holiday in Australia, where I was visiting my youngest daughter, Sharon, a butterfly flew onto the altar and everyone turned round and smiled at me. They also gave me a farewell card with butterflies on it. That was also in late October. I told this story to my daughter in Australia and as I went through customs at Sydney airport a red admiral landed on my shoulder. A few days later we went to Mass together and another landed on our pew. We shared a very special moment together.

As I was leaving Australia a butterfly flew past me in the departure lounge and on my first Sunday after I had returned home and was attending Mass, a butterfly flew down onto the altar. This was in January. The same day my other daughter, Deborah, was gathering logs for the fire in the wheelbarrow when one settled on the barrow.

On July 12th two years later, a beautiful stained glass window that had been created for Peter by Helen O'Connor (whose husband John had been at school with Peter) was dedicated, and many of his friends who had worshipped at Our Lady of Consolation, West Grinstead were there. I went up to the lectern to tell people about the significance of the window when (unbeknown to me) a butterfly circled my head and soared up to it.

A week later, at my daughter Deborrah's wedding in the same church, a red admiral flew over the couple's heads. It also appeared in the marquee at 1 p.m., captured on video during the reception.

A few weeks later I was visiting Helen as it was her daughter's

21st birthday. We were all having a sing-song round the piano when someone called out, "Look, a moth"; but, no, of course it was a butterfly! I spent the night there and next day there was one in the shower room and another in my bedroom. This was in November!

I met my second husband, Michael, when he attended the special Mass mentioned above, when the window to Peter's memory was dedicated. Michael was amazed at the number of people attending. He usually attended Mass on a Saturday evening and I always went on Sundays. He started coming on Sundays and we met up over coffee afterwards in the church. Eight years later we were married and at our reception a red admiral flew into the marquee and over our heads. Many of our friends took great pleasure in seeing this as I had told them of my experiences of butterflies. Peter and the angels have sent Michael to me, of that I am sure.

In recent years we have been very blessed by having the opportunity to design and build a beautiful stone house with magnificent views on a remote Greek island. In our first week of occupation a brown and yellow butterfly flew in to greet us.

P.S. I was reading *Angel Inspiration*, a gift from my daughter in law, by Diana Cooper, who said that the Archangel Michael looks after people born under the sign of Leo. That is Michael. I read this and said, "Archangel Michael, send your sign to Michael." I could not believe it when Michael called me and said, "Darling, a robin just ran under my chair and is sitting in the tree." We had never ever seen a robin in Greece at any time! Another appeared and they stayed a couple of days! I told Michael that the robin is his angel and he believed me!

Angels Come in Dreams

I once had a very vivid dream after Peter died, which gave me great comfort. It depicted a barren desert-like scene and a winding road and I could see a great barefooted crowd approaching wearing white clothes with Peter at the head, though he was wearing a sports jacket but no shoes. I had been driving through a crowded town in an open topped sports car (I have never had one nor wanted one, incidentally) and felt tired and confused so stopped to watch the crowd approaching. As he drew near he climbed in and said to me, "I have never been so happy." He then put his arms round me and said, "I'll be there whenever you may need me" and then he got out of the car and smiled back at me as he joyfully rejoined the procession. Later, at a friend's house, I saw a painting of a desert-like scene which was the exact replica of my dream. I really wanted to buy it!

Butterflies are rarer these days, sometimes appearing at particular times of great happiness and maybe Peter knows I am safe and content. Mike and I are now 'living the dream'. The angels have certainly been with us all along.

Lightning Source UK Ltd.
Milton Keynes UK
UKHW040913050122
396655UK00005B/377

9 781909 477100